BARNYARD
BANTER

For Laura Godwin,
 My Bantering Buddy

ISBN 0-590-20307-X

Copyright © 1994 by Denise Fleming.
All rights reserved.
Published by Scholastic Inc., 555 Broadway, New York, NY 10012, by arrangement with Henry Holt and Company, Inc.

12 11 10 9   8 9/9 0/0
Printed in the U.S.A.   14

First Scholastic printing, February 1995

BARNYARD BANTER

Denise Fleming

Scholastic Inc. New York Toronto London Auckland Sydney

cows in the pasture,
moo,
moo,
moo

Roosters in the barnyard,

cock-a-doodle-doo

Hens in the henhouse,

cluck,

cluck,

cluck

Pigs in the wallow,

muck,

muck,

muck

But where's Goose?

Kittens in the hayloft,

mew, mew, mew mew

Pigeons
in the rafters,

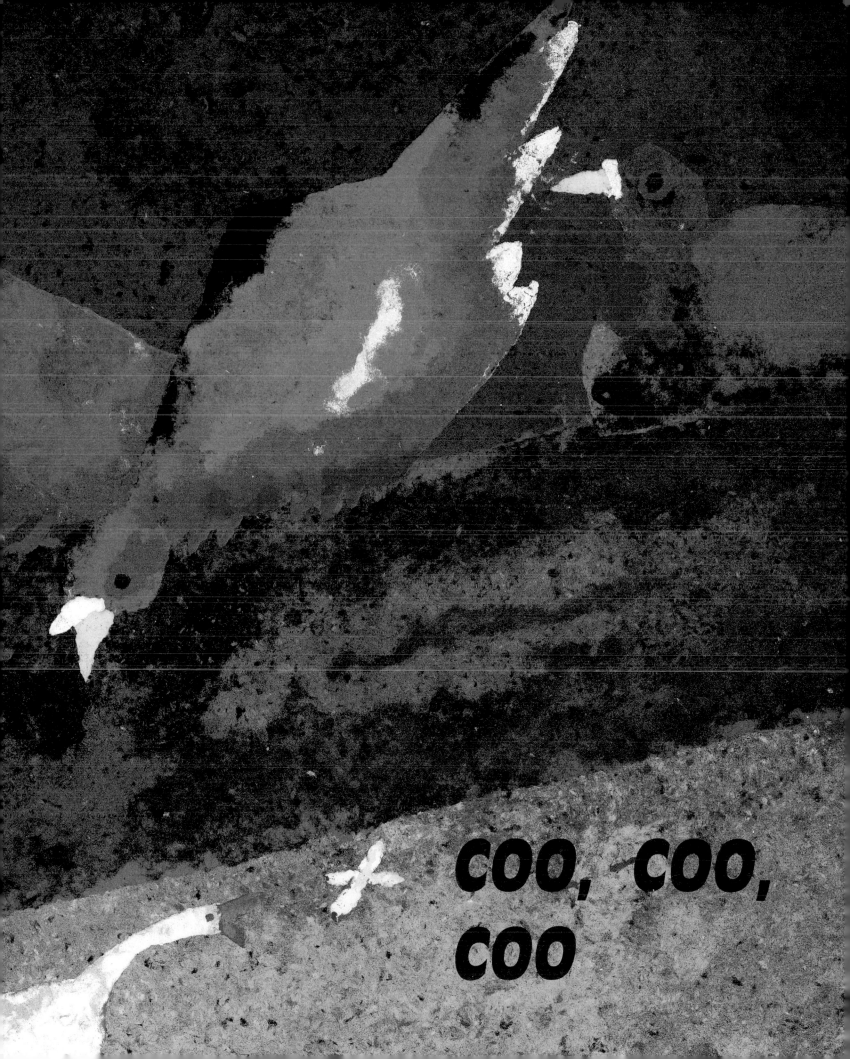

COO, COO,
COO

Mice
in the grain bin,

squeak,
squeak,

Peacocks in the wire pen,

Donkeys in the paddock,

Crows
in the cornfield,

caw,

caw,

caw

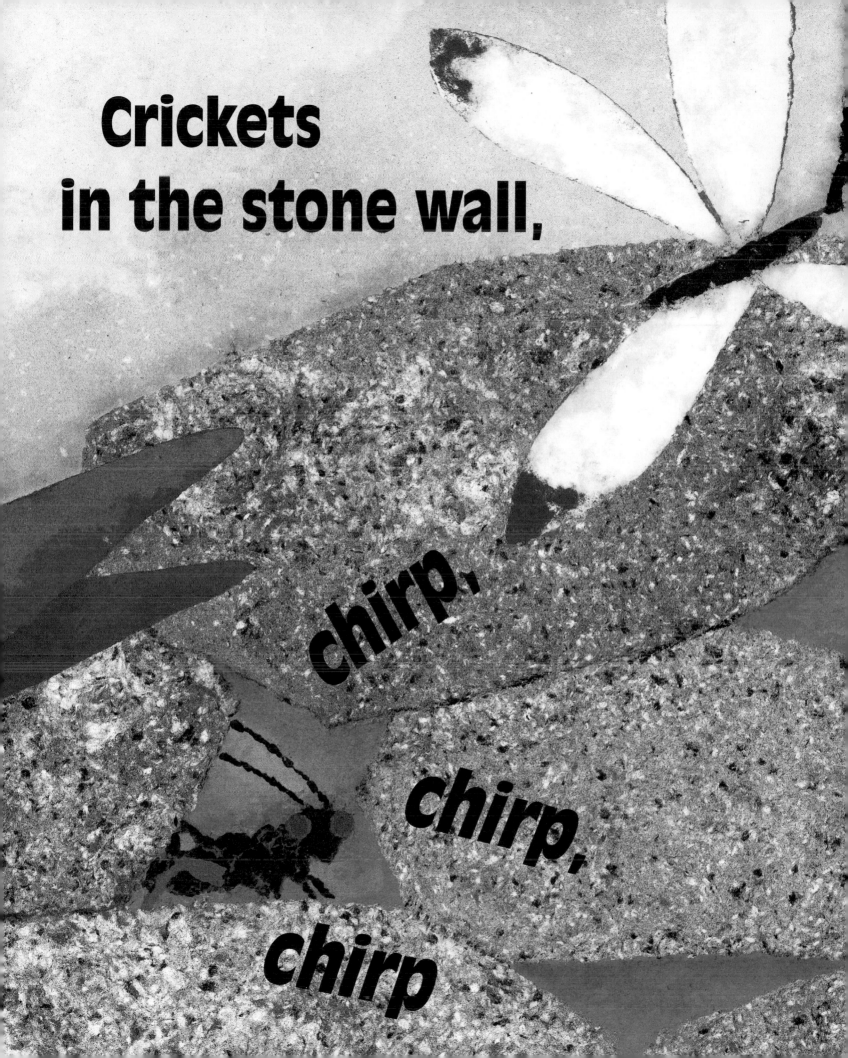

Crickets
in the stone wall,

chirp,

chirp,

chirp

Frogs
in the farm pond,

burp, burp, burp

But where's Goose?

moo, moo, moo

cock -a- doodle -doo

cluck, cluck, cluck

muck, muck, muck

mew, mew, mew

coo, coo, coo

squeak, squeak, squeak

shriek, shriek, shriek

hee, haw, haw

caw, caw, caw

chirp, chirp, chirp

burp, burp, burp

But where's
Goose?

There's Goose!

honk, honk, honk